With special thanks to Cherith Baldry

To Sarah

www.beastquest.co.uk

ORCHARD BOOKS
338 Euston Road, London NW1 3BH
Orchard Books Australia
Level 17/207 Kent St, Sydney, NSW 2000

A Paperback Original
First published in Great Britain in 2007

Beast Quest is a registered trademark of Beast Quest Limited
Series created by Working Partners Limited, London

Text © Beast Quest Limited 2009
Cover illustration © David Wyatt 2007
Inside illustrations © Orchard Books 2007

ISBN 978 1 84616 486 6

17
Printed in Great Britain by J. F. Print Ltd, Sparkford.

The paper and board used in this paperback are natural recyclable
products made from wood grown in sustainable forests. The
manufacturing processes conform to the environmental regulations of
the country of origin.

Orchard Books is a division of Hachette Children's Books,
an Hachette UK company.

www.hachette.co.uk

TAGUS
THE HORSE-MAN

BY ADAM BLADE

ORCHARD BOOKS

THE ICY

THE

THE NORTHERN
MOUNTAINS

WESTERN OCEAN

THE FOREST
OF FEAR

TH

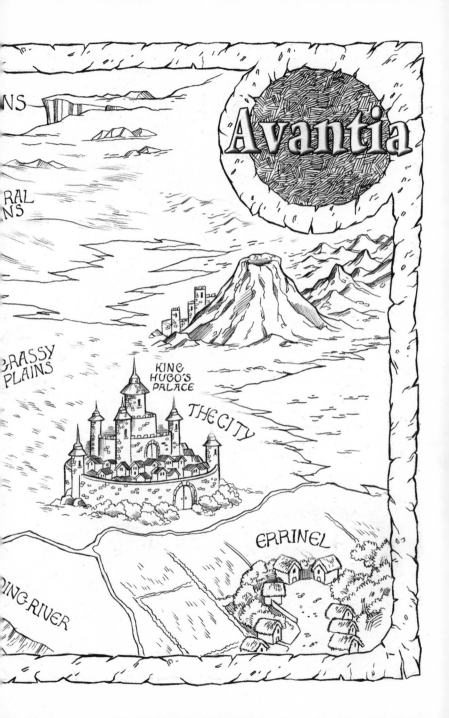

*W*elcome to the kingdom of Avantia. I am Aduro – a good wizard residing in the palace of King Hugo. You join us at a difficult time. Let me explain...

It is written in the Ancient Scripts that our peaceful kingdom shall one day be plunged into peril.

Now that time has come.

Under the evil spell of Malvel the Dark Wizard, six Beasts – fire dragon, sea serpent, mountain giant, horse-man, snow monster and flame bird – run wild and destroy the land they once protected.

Avantia is in great danger.

The Ancient Scripts also predict an unlikely hero. It is written that a boy shall take up the Quest to free the Beasts from the curse and save the kingdom.

We do not know who this boy is, only that his time has come...

We pray our young hero will have the courage and the heart to take up the Quest. Will you join us as we wait and watch?

Avantia salutes you,

Aduro

PROLOGUE

Victor woke with a start. Grabbing
his sword, he sat up and looked
round wildly. It was just before dawn
and the sky was beginning to lighten
in the east. The coals from last
night's campfire were still glowing.
Victor surveyed the shadowy plains
and the herd of cattle. Nothing
seemed out of the ordinary.

"Must have been a bad dream,"
he thought, and settled back onto
his bedroll.

But he couldn't sleep. In the last week, there had been three attacks on cattle during the night. In the last attack, four calves had been killed. No one knew who or what was responsible. Victor wasn't sure what to think, but he was certainly glad the night was almost over. He only had to keep watch over the herd until the morning. The men were all asleep beside their own campfires, away from the cattle.

He listened to the sounds of the plains. There was a slight breeze rustling the tall grasses and he could hear the last of the crickets chirping softly. Then a bird called out over the lowing cattle.

Wait a minute...that wasn't right. The cattle should be sleeping, not lowing!

Sitting up, Victor looked closely at

his herd. The cattle were huddled together more tightly than usual, with their calves grouped in the centre – a sign that they felt threatened. But why?

Just then Victor heard the sound of hooves drumming in the distance. Was it just his imagination?

The cattle began to stamp restlessly. Victor leapt to his feet. The hoofbeats were growing closer!

Something was out there.

Then a large shape loomed out of the darkness in front of him. Suddenly, standing before him in the red glow of the campfire was a horrifying Beast.

Victor gasped. The monster had the torso of a giant man, but it was attached to the body of a powerful stallion!

Stumbling back in terror, Victor

stared up at the creature. His dark hair and beard were wildly tangled, and the reflection from the campfire had turned his black eyes a flaming, angry red.

The Beast reared up on its hind legs, grunting fiercely, its hooves pounding the air. With a sense of panic, Victor realised it was going to charge!

He tried to dive out of the way. But he wasn't fast enough. One of the Beast's hooves struck him on the head, knocking him to the ground. Then the Beast galloped through the fire, scattering the red-hot coals in a flurry of sparks. It flung its head back and roared as the dry grass of the plains began to catch fire.

Dazed, Victor saw the creature charge towards the helpless, frantic cattle...

Then the pain overcame him and everything went black.

CHAPTER ONE

A THOUSAND HOOVES

"I think that was the biggest challenge yet," said Tom.

He sat tall in his saddle as he rode from the northern mountains of Avantia on his black horse, Storm. His friend Elenna sat behind him as she usually did, her arms around his waist. Tom had just freed Arcta the mountain giant from the evil spell of

Malvel the Dark Wizard, and they were all tired. But Storm bravely pressed on, with Silver, Elenna's tame wolf, padding quietly after them. It was mid-afternoon and the sun was strong.

"I thought I'd be trapped in that cave for ever," Elenna agreed. "Arcta was so angry!"

"I'd be angry too if an evil wizard had enslaved me!" Tom said. He gave a sigh of satisfaction. "But Arcta is free now. There will be no more trouble."

"Not from him," Elenna pointed out. "But we have a new Beast Quest now. How long do you think it will take to reach the central plains?"

"Not long," said Tom. "I just hope we're ready for the next test." He touched the hilt of his sword, and was reminded of the challenges he had faced so far: Ferno the fire dragon,

Sepron the sea serpent, Arcta the mountain giant... Once more he thought about his father, Taladon the Swift, and wondered if he would be proud of what he had achieved on this Quest. He hoped so. His father had disappeared when Tom was a baby, but somehow he felt he knew him.

"While there is blood in my veins," he thought, "I will not let my father down!" Then he remembered that King Hugo and his adviser Wizard Aduro had trusted him with this Quest – he didn't want to let them down, either.

"I know you can do it," Elenna said, giving him a playful jab. "And don't forget, you've got me to protect you."

Tom glanced over his shoulder and smiled. "I haven't forgotten. I'm really glad we met! I'd never have made it this far without you."

He brought Storm to a halt and pulled out his magical map from his pocket. Elenna peered over his shoulder. A glowing red line showed the road from the mountains of the north to the central plains, which were surrounded by a ridge of hills. Tiny cattle moved about on the plains, where there was rich grass for them to eat.

"I think we're about here." Tom pointed to the edge of the hills on the map. "It can't be too far now."

He put the map away and, with a nudge of his heels, urged Storm on. "We're getting close," he said. "We should keep an eye out for the next Beast."

"Wizard Aduro said he's half-man, half-horse," Elenna said, shivering.

Tom nodded. "Tagus. He's attacking the cattle on the plains. With no cattle the people who live there will have little to eat and nothing to trade. They could starve."

"And so could the rest of the kingdom," Elenna added anxiously.

Tom tightened his grip on the reins. Storm whinnied, as if he knew what they were up against. Tom patted his horse's neck. With each Quest, their bond grew stronger.

Soon they came to the crest of a low hill. Tom reined in Storm and looked out across the wide plains, which stretched as far as he could see. He could see the long grasses swaying in the breeze. A river wound through clumps of trees. In the distance, a lake glinted in the sunlight. Silver's ears pricked up and he sniffed the air eagerly.

"It's beautiful!" Elenna exclaimed. "Maybe Wizard Aduro sent us here before Tagus had the chance to do terrible damage."

"Could be." Tom's heartbeat quickened with hope. In the south, the crops had been burned by Ferno the fire dragon. In the west, Sepron the sea serpent had flooded the coast. Arcta the mountain giant had nearly destroyed the northern mountains with landslides. Tom had almost forgotten what ordinary, peaceful countryside looked like. "Look over there," he said, pointing into the distance. He could just make out square grey towers and rooftops covered with red tiles. "That must be the town."

"Then let's go!" said Elenna.

Storm cantered down the hill towards the plains. Tom enjoyed the steady beat of his hooves, sensing his horse's rising excitement. Silver let

out a joyful yelp and sprang ahead of
them. He disappeared into the long
grass until all Tom and Elenna could
see of him was the tip of his tail.

On the breeze Tom could smell
a hint of smoke, as if a campfire were
burning nearby. He scanned the
horizon to see if he could catch sight
of it. But all he could see was a herd
of cattle, moving towards them in
a thick mass.

As they watched, Tom and Elenna

began to sense that something was wrong.

The herd wasn't walking peacefully. They were stampeding!

"They're heading right for us!" cried Tom.

"Silver!" Elenna yelled frantically. She let out a piercing whistle, and within seconds the grey wolf was bounding through the tall grass towards them.

Tom kicked Storm's flanks once more, and the horse took off across the plains in the direction of the town, galloping as fast as he could, with Silver sprinting just behind.

But the stampeding herd was

gaining on them. Dust began to fill the air, and the pounding of hooves on the hard ground was deafening.

Tom looked over his shoulder. The herd was much larger then he had thought. There must have been a thousand massive animals, each the size of a large boulder. They were charging blindly, trampling anything that stood in their way. The ground was shaking under their weight.

"Hurry, Storm!" Tom yelled above the roar of the stampede.

He bent his head into Storm's mane, and could feel Elenna gripping onto him as they flew across the plains towards the town. Suddenly Storm skidded to a stop.

"Go, Storm! Keep going!" Tom yelled. "We're almost there—"

Then he heard a crackling sound and looked up. Instantly, he knew why Storm had halted.

In front of them was a wall of fire.
The dry grass of the plains had been
set alight – and it was spreading
swiftly.

They were trapped!

CHAPTER TWO

TRAPPED!

There was nowhere to go. The only thing they could do was turn and run with the stampeding cattle. It was risky, but they had no choice. Tom's shield, which protected him from fire, would not be able to defend the four of them.

Tom wheeled Storm round, and the brave horse ran back towards the mass of cattle. Soon he was running alongside the herd, then right in the middle of it, with Silver running close beside him for protection.

Choking on the dust and smoke, Tom urged Storm on. "Go, boy! Go!"

After a quarter of a mile, they had outrun the spreading fire – for the moment.

"Left!" Tom yelled, pulling on Storm's reins.

The horse made an abrupt turn, breaking from the stampede, Silver following him as if he were Storm's shadow.

Tom eased the stallion to a stop just before a hill. "We need to make a firebreak, to stop the fire from reaching the town!" he yelled above the thundering hooves of the cattle, as they faded into the distance.

He jumped down from Storm's back. "Get Silver and Storm behind that hill!" he called to Elenna as he ran towards the approaching flames.

As Elenna urged the animals to safety, Tom began chopping the tall grass with his sword. He knew if he could clear a wide enough break in front of the fire's path, it would have nowhere to go.

Holding his shield in front of himself, he cleared a large swathe of grass, knowing that the dragon scale in his shield would keep him safe from the blaze. He swung his sword again and again until the flames had nothing left to consume and began to die down.

As the fire flickered out, Tom collapsed to the ground in exhaustion. His face was covered in soot, and he was coughing from all the smoke.

Anxiously Elena ran towards him. She handed him some water and bread, then crouched in the long grass beside him.

Tom ate and drank a little, but he felt restless, as if the danger was not yet over. "We'd better get moving," he said as soon as he'd finished. He staggered up.

A shout rang out. "There he is!"

Tom looked up to see a band of men approaching from the direction of the town.

"Get him!" another man shouted.

Tom clutched his sword and shield.

"Elenna, I don't think they've seen you," he said quickly. "Get back to Storm and Silver, and take them to safety."

She cast him a worried look, but they were used to acting as a team now, so she immediately crawled through the long grass back to the hill. Tom knew she would be there for him when it counted.

He did his best to look calm.

Soon the jostling mob surrounded him. It was made up of big men, and they were brandishing scythes and pitchforks. Their faces were red with anger. There were too many of them to fight.

"Why are they so furious?" Tom wondered. All he'd done was save their town from a wildfire.

"Wait a minute. I haven't done anything wrong—" he began.

But no one was listening to him.

One of the men pushed forward and grabbed him by the shoulder. "Where's Victor?" he demanded.

Then everyone seemed to be shouting at once. "Look – he's covered in soot! He must have started the fire."

"And what about our cattle?" Another man thrust his face close to Tom's, glaring fiercely at him. "You've made them stampede."

Someone else struck Tom a powerful blow that knocked the air from him. "Our families will starve!"

"Who's Victor? I don't know what you're talking about," Tom sputtered, trying to get his wind back.

But the men were shouting and Tom couldn't make himself heard. Fear surged up inside him as they crowded round. He gripped his sword and shield tightly, but one of the men wrenched them out of his hands.

Then another voice rang out. "Wait! Let me talk to him." A tall man pushed his way to the front of the crowd. His face was stern.

The crowd moved back and the shouts died down to angry muttering.

"I'm Adam, the head guard of the town," the tall man said. "My son Victor disappeared from a camp near here. He was helping to look after a herd of cattle. Do you know anything about him?"

Tom's heart pounded as he looked at the angry faces around him. "No, I don't," he said. "I've only just come down from the north. I barely escaped the stampede myself. I'm the one that put out the fire." He glanced round at the circle of suspicious faces and added, "You've got to let me go. I have something really important to do."

"I'll bet!" one of the men jeered.

"Don't believe him," said another.

Two men grabbed his arms, pulling him in different directions.

"So you won't tell the truth, eh?" someone else called out. "We'll soon see about that!"

CHAPTER THREE

BEHIND BARS

By the time Tom and the crowd reached the town, the sun had set. The streets were dark and narrow with overhanging roofs that hid the sky. Rubbish lay scattered around empty market stalls, and stray dogs picked among the scraps.

Adam and the other men marched Tom through the streets. Tom tried to pull away, but it was no use. These men were twice his size, and very strong.

"Why won't you listen to me?" Tom pleaded. "I don't know anything about your son."

"Then tell me, why are you here?" Adam asked him. "And what's so important about what you have to do?"

"I can't tell you that," he answered. Tom had promised Wizard Aduro and King Hugo that he would keep his Beast Quest secret.

"Then you give me no choice," said Adam, shrugging.

The band of men stopped outside a big stone building. Two guards stood by the door. Tom began to panic as he realised where he was.

"No!" he cried. "You can't put me in prison!"

Still keeping a firm grip on Tom's

shoulder, Adam turned to face the rest of the men. "Go back to your homes," he ordered. "I'll see that justice is done. If the boy knows anything about Victor, I'll find out."

The men shuffled away, giving Tom angry looks as they went.

Adam pushed open the door and thrust Tom inside. One of the guards followed.

Tom found himself in a large bare room lit by an oil lamp hanging from a beam. In the middle of the room was an old wooden table and chair. The guard pushed Tom across the room and through an inner door into a long, stone-flagged passage. Another lamp hung from the ceiling. On either side of the passage were heavy iron doors. Tom felt his stomach tighten with fear.

The guard unhooked a bunch of

keys from his belt and opened the door at the end of the passage. Then he grabbed Tom by the arm and threw him inside. Tom sprawled onto the filthy floor, then climbed awkwardly to his feet, rubbing his elbow. He was in a prison cell!

"I'll question you in the morning," said Adam gruffly. "A night in the cells should loosen your tongue."

The cell door slammed shut and the guard turned the key. Tom heard

the two men walk away, their footsteps muffled by the heavy door.

He looked round his cell. The walls and floor were made of stone and there were no windows. Along one wall was a wooden bench with a single, tattered blanket. It smelled foul. Tom shivered.

"Now what do I do?" he wondered. He knew that he was in real danger if he couldn't prove his innocence. And then he wouldn't be able to save Avantia from Tagus the horse-man!

He must free the Beast from Malvel's curse – as well as making sure that Elenna, Silver and Storm were safe. But first he had to escape!

CHAPTER FOUR

HOOFBEATS IN THE NIGHT

Tom paced the cell. "There has to be a way out," he thought. He patted the stones against the outside wall with the palm of his hand, listening carefully for any weak spots, which would sound hollow. But they were all solid, held together with a mixture of dried tar and rock flakes. It would be impossible to chip any part of it away without a chisel. Tom sat down on the bench feeling helpless.

Then an idea hit him. If he could get the guard to bring him some food, the door would have to be opened, if only for a moment.

Tom walked over and examined the door. When the key was turned, a bolt slid from inside the door into a hole in the wall. As he looked closer, Tom's thoughts were interrupted by a drop of water. And another. He looked up. There was a steady drip coming from the ceiling. He glanced back at the lock. Over the years the dripping water had worn a gap between the wall and the door – just wide enough for Tom's fingers to slip through. Tom tapped at the stone. It wasn't very strong. The water had obviously weakened it. "I wonder..." he thought.

Tom tore a strip of cloth from his shirt. He knew what to do. He would have to be quick, but it might just work.

The moment the door was unlocked, he would stuff the fabric into the hole. Then, when the guard locked the door again, the bolt would force the fabric against the stone. With any luck, it would be enough to crumble the weakened rock.

When he felt sure he could do it, he called out to the guard as loudly as he could. "Hello! Hello!"

He listened as the guard's heavy footsteps came down the corridor.

"What is it, boy?" he asked roughly.

"I'm hungry," Tom said.

"Then you'll have to wait till

morning," the guard replied cruelly.

"But I haven't eaten in days!" Tom hated lying, but he had no choice. He had to get out.

"Then eat your shoe!" The guard laughed, clearly taking pleasure in being mean.

"You have to feed me," Tom yelled. "It's the law of Avantia that you treat prisoners with dignity!"

Tom listened as the footsteps made their way back down the corridor. He waited with his ear to the door.

A few moments later, he heard the guard returning. Tom readied himself, placing his fingers in the space between the door and the wall. The footsteps stopped before the door and he heard the guard fiddling with the keys. This was it!

Tom felt the bolt slide back into the door as the guard turned the key. As

quickly as he could, he pushed the
piece of cloth into the hole in the
wall. Just as he did so, the door
swung open and hit him on the
forehead, sending him flying.

The guard stomped in as Tom lay
sprawled on the ground.

"Trying to escape, eh?" the guard
laughed, looking down at Tom with
a crooked-toothed grin. "There's no
escaping from here, lad." Then he
dropped a plate of cold gruel on the
stone floor and stomped back out of

the cell, pulling the door closed behind him.

As the guard turned the lock, Tom heard the faint clink of stones falling on the floor of the cell. His plan had worked!

Tom waited until the footsteps had completely disappeared before daring to move towards the front of the cell. When he was sure the guard had gone, he pulled gently on the door. The rest of the stone crumbled around the bolt, and the door opened!

Tom peeked his head out and checked there were no other guards. When he was sure the coast was clear, he stepped into the stone-flagged passage and shut the cell door carefully behind him. Then he crept towards the big door at the end of the passage, listening carefully.

Everything was silent. At last he dared to edge the door open and peered through the crack. The room was empty and in darkness. No guards were there.

Tom slid into the room and closed the door behind him. Then he froze. The latch on the outer door was being lifted!

Tom darted for the only hiding place he could see – a dark archway in one wall. The outer door swung open and another guard appeared. "I'll just check on the prisoners," he said to someone outside.

He tramped across the room and through the door to the cells. Tom's stomach dropped. He only had a few minutes before the guard would discover that he was missing! He had to hurry. But there was another guard outside the front door. He couldn't escape that way.

Then he realised he was standing at the foot of a spiral staircase. He had no idea where it led, but it was the only way to go. He climbed up, clutching the rope that was looped along the wall.

Groping in the darkness, Tom felt a wooden frame in the stone wall. "It must be a window," he thought. There were shutters, he realised, but they were closed. Tom fumbled with the catch and swung them open.

Just then the guard called out. "The boy is gone!"

The other guard shouted frantically, "Over here! Maybe he went up here!"

Tom heard both men start up the staircase. He had to get out. Now!

In the moonlight, Tom saw that the window led out onto a small balcony. He climbed out of the window and

peered over the rail down to the street.
There were no other guards in sight;
this must be the back of the prison.

He thought he might be able to
climb down, but the wall was sheer

and there was nothing to hold on to.
"Now what?" he asked himself.

He had to get down fast. He would
have to risk climbing over the
balcony rail and letting himself drop
into the street – but he didn't dare
think what would happen if he broke
a leg. Tom wished he still had his
shield. Since he freed Arcta, it had

the power to protect him when
jumping or falling from great heights.

He was gripping the rail of the
balcony, getting ready to swing
himself over, when he heard a sound
slicing through the darkness. His
heart almost stopped.

Slow hoofbeats were echoing in the
silence of the night. And they were
coming towards him!

CHAPTER FIVE

VICTOR

Could it be Tagus? Would the Beast really dare come into the town?

Tom crouched behind the balcony rail and peered down into the street again. A shape appeared out of the shadows. Tom grinned with relief as he recognised the horse and its rider. It was Elenna and Storm! And Silver was there, too.

"Elenna!" he called softly.

She halted the horse just below the balcony and looked up. "Tom! Are you all right?" she whispered back.

"I'm fine. Just help me get out of here."

Elenna unfastened a rope from the saddle. "Catch," she said, tossing it to him.

Tom grabbed the end and tied it around the balcony rail. Then he hesitated, looking back through the window. Somewhere inside were his sword and shield. He didn't want to leave without them. But he could hear the guards running up the spiral staircase behind him.

"Come on," Elenna urged him.

Tom knew he had no choice. He swung himself over the balcony rail just as the guards appeared at the window.

"There he is! Get him!" they cried as he climbed down the rope, dropping neatly onto Storm's back.

"*Go!*" he yelled.

They rode through the dark, empty streets and out onto the plains.

"After they took you, I didn't know what to do," Elenna said, once they had left the town behind. "I took Storm and Silver to the lake and made a camp there. I was so worried. But I knew I should wait until dark to come and help."

"You came at just the right time," Tom said. "I couldn't have escaped without you."

The plains were quiet and still. It was a clear night, and the moon and stars gave enough light for them to make their way back to the camp. They could see the surface of the lake shimmering in the moonlight.

Tom looked over his shoulder. "No one is following us," he said, relieved.

Then, in the quiet of the night, they heard a whimper. Elenna brought

Storm to a stop. Tom scanned the darkness, listening closely. Silver whined anxiously. The sound was coming from some bushes up ahead.

Tom scrambled down from Storm and rushed over to the bushes. Elenna followed, leading Storm by the reins, Silver at her heels. Crouching on the ground was a boy with a huge purple bruise on his face.

"Who are you?" Tom asked.

"M-m-my name's Victor," the boy stuttered. He was clearly in pain.

"Victor!" Tom cried. "Are you Adam's son?"

The boy nodded.

Tom couldn't believe it. "Your father has been looking everywhere for you!" he said.

"I was helping to look after the cattle," Victor explained. He swallowed, clenching his fists as if remembering something terrible. "We'd all heard the stories about the horse-man who kept attacking the cattle. Last night I was keeping watch – and I saw him."

"Really?" Elenna asked. She and Tom exchanged worried glances.

"Yes," Victor replied. "When I was young, my mother told me about Tagus the horse-man, who keeps watch over the herds. I always thought that was just a fairy story, like the rest of the Beasts in Avantia. But he wasn't there to protect us last night. I was terrified! I know it sounds unbelievable, but he really is half-man and half-horse. He reared up and charged – and one of his hooves hit me on the head. It knocked me out. When I woke, there was a fire and the cattle were stampeding. I ran, trying to get away, but I tripped and fell. I think I've broken my leg," Victor winced, touching his leg gingerly.

Tom looked at Elenna. Victor was lucky to be alive.

"We saw the fire and the stampede," he said. "It's too dangerous to travel at night, so we'll sleep here then take you back to town first thing tomorrow."

Between them they helped Victor

hobble to their camp by the lake. They cooked some fish that Elenna had caught, then they settled down for the night. They were all exhausted.

Tom gazed out into the darkness. Nothing. He tried to sleep.

But the sounds of the plains were unfamiliar and kept him awake. The long grasses rustled in the night breeze and crickets chirped to one another.

Then there was another sound. A low, distant moaning that made Tom shiver. He sat up sharply and listened. There it was again! But this time the moan sounded angry. Was it Tagus?

They didn't have much time to free the Beast from Malvel's evil spell. Soon there would be another attack, and someone could be seriously hurt – or even killed.

Tom waited and listened for a while longer. But whatever it was had gone.

CHAPTER SIX

BACK TO THE TOWN

Dawn light spread across the plains as Tom and Elenna packed up the camp.

"There's no time for breakfast," Tom said, as he and Elenna lifted Victor onto Storm's saddle. "We need to get going right now."

The boy's condition wasn't good – he could hardly talk. They had to get him to a doctor as soon as possible.

They reached the town as the sun rose. Tom was riding Storm with Victor slumped in the saddle behind him, while Elenna walked alongside with Silver. It was so early that the streets should have been empty. But there were clusters of people whispering amongst themselves. Some were weeping.

Tom pulled Storm to a halt. "What is it?" he asked a young man.

"What's wrong?"

The man turned and peered up at Tom, shielding his eyes against the early morning sun. He looked angry. "Another herd of cattle stampeded in the night," he man said. He spat on the ground in disgust. "Two villages have been completely destroyed."

Just then, another man called out, "It's him again!"

All at once, every person turned

and looked at Tom.

"And he's got Victor!" called out another.

Before Tom knew it, he was once more surrounded by an angry mob. Men were waving weapons and yelling at the top of their lungs.

Hearing the commotion, a guard approached the crowd. Seeing Tom, he drew his sword and called to the other guards at the prison. "It's the boy who's been causing the stampedes."

Someone grabbed Storm's reins and another pulled Victor from the saddle. Victor let out a cry of pain. Before he had a chance to flee, Tom, too, was dragged from Storm's back.

"What's going on here?" came a gruff voice from the edge of the mob. It was Adam the head guard. The people quietened down as Adam made his way to where Tom was

being held by two large men.

"It's the boy that escaped," a guard said. "And he's got your son."

Adam looked at Victor lying in the dirt. A woman was trying to comfort him as he writhed and winced in agony. "Victor!" he cried. "You're safe!" He ran to the boy and held him in his arms. Then he turned to Tom, his eyes narrowing in fierce anger.

"What have you done?" he thundered. "What have you done to my boy?"

"Wait!" Victor's voice was choked with pain. "It's not Tom's fault. Tom didn't cause the stampedes. He saved me."

A murmur went through the crowd. The townspeople were silent as they looked at Adam for his reaction.

"Release the boy," he said. "And someone get the doctor." Then he looked at Tom. "I'm sorry," he said. "I was wrong to lock you up." He gazed out at the crowd of people and their worried faces. "We've had other things to worry about since then," he added quietly. He held out a hand and Tom shook it. "You deserve a reward," he went on. "Ask for whatever you want. You brought my son back."

"I don't want a reward," Tom replied, "just my sword and shield."

Adam nodded to one of the guards, who dashed into the prison and reappeared carrying the sword and shield. He gave them to Tom with a smile.

"Thank you," Tom said. He fitted the sword into its sheath and slung the shield over his shoulder. Now he was ready to face Tagus.

But he still didn't know how to find the horse-man. Then something occurred to Tom. Maybe he didn't have to go after the Beast. Maybe, if he helped to look after the cattle, the Beast would find him!

"Let my friends and I lend a hand on the next cattle drive," Tom suggested to Adam. "If you have more people to keep watch over the herd, you might have a better chance of keeping it safe." He exchanged a glance with Elenna, who was standing quietly with Silver at the edge of the crowd.

"That's a generous offer," Adam said. "But it's risky. I don't know if we ought to ask you…"

A broad, red-faced man pushed his way to the front of the crowd. "Me and my neighbour are taking our cattle south tomorrow," he announced. "It's the biggest drive of the season. We're going to the city to sell the cattle at the market there. We'll be glad of your help." He paused, giving Silver a doubtful look. "That's a powerful big dog you've got there. It *is* a dog, isn't it?" he added nervously.

"He's a wolf," said Elenna cheerfully. "But don't worry. He's well-trained. He won't harm your cattle."

"Maybe he'll sink his teeth into the horse-man," said a voice from the crowd.

"Let's hope so," Elenna muttered to Tom.

Adam nodded, as if he had made up his mind. "Then it's settled," he said to Tom and Elenna. "You'll leave tomorrow at dawn."

CHAPTER SEVEN

THE CATTLE DRIVE

The next morning, Adam guided
Tom and Elenna to the edge of town.
The cattle drive was ready to set out.
A crowd of townspeople had
gathered to see the cattlemen and
the herd on their way. Yapping dogs
dashed up and down, and children
called out excitedly.

Tom gazed in amazement at the

huge number of cattle milling about on the plains. The air was filled with the sound of their lowing and the soft clang of the bells round their necks.

Slowly the herd began to move off. There were huge beasts with shaggy black coats and curving horns, as well as young calves, trotting beside their mothers.

Men rode on horses alongside the herd. Children from the town ran after them. "Goodbye!" they

called. "And good luck!"

Tom, Elenna, Storm and Silver found a place near the back of the herd. At home in his village, Tom had often thought it would be fun to join one of the great cattle drives. Now he had his wish, and he wasn't thinking about having fun at all. He just wanted to find Tagus and release him from Malvel's curse.

Gradually the walls and towers of the town disappeared behind them.

Tom began to get used to the smell and the noise of the herd. Just in front of them, Silver was running along the edge of the herd, drawing ahead and then bounding back with yelps of excitement. Some of the calves shied away nervously. But as the day went on, the cattle became used to Silver. They moved at the same slow pace, dust swirling around their hooves.

Tom kept scanning the horizon, but he couldn't see any sign of Tagus. Then he caught sight of deep hoof-prints in a damp patch of ground.

"Look!" he whispered to Elenna, who was sitting behind him on Storm as usual. "Tagus has been here."

Elenna frowned. "It could be one of the cattlemen's horses."

"No, these prints are huge!" Tom shivered. "I think the Beast must be very close by."

The sun was going down when the herd gradually slowed to a halt. "We're making camp," one of the men told them as he rode by. "There's a river up ahead where the cattle can drink."

Urging Storm on, Tom and Elenna skirted the edge of the herd until they reached the river. A muddy slope, churned up by many hooves, led down to the water. Here and there, the men were beginning to make campfires. The cattle pressed forward to get to the river and drink.

"Let's make our fire over there," Elenna suggested, pointing upstream to where trees grew close to the water's edge. "It's away from the herd and the men. We can keep an eye out for Tagus."

"Good idea," Tom agreed.

Tom and Elenna made their way
upstream. Beyond the trees, on the
other side of the river, the ground
sloped upward and the lush grass of
the plains gave way to bare rock.

They made a fire at the edge of the
river. The leaping scarlet flames
glowed in the twilight. Tom peered
past the flames and out across the
plains. But there was no sign of the
horse-man. The darkness was dotted
with the red glow of other campfires.

"One of us will have to stay
awake," he said. "You try to get some
sleep, and I'll take the first watch."

"All right." Elenna lay down by the
fire with Silver. "Don't forget to
wake me."

Tom scrambled up the tallest tree and
found a fork in the branches where

he could sit and look out over the plains. A half-moon was shining through thin clouds. Beyond the camp, nothing disturbed the darkness. He could hardly make out the herd among the shadows and mist.

Hours went by, but Tom still saw nothing. The sky in the east grew pale as dawn approached. The danger seemed to be over for another night. He was about to climb down from the tree when he spotted a black outline where the sky was the brightest, right opposite him on the other side of the river.

"Tagus!" Tom whispered under his breath.

At last!

Then the Beast stepped towards the riverbank out of the mist. Tom gasped. He was a huge, terrifying figure, half-man and half-horse. As

Tom stared in horror, the creature reared, hooves striking out at the air, and gave a battle cry that echoed across the plains.

Elenna sat up quickly, pushing her hair out of her eyes. "What was that?"

Then the Beast disappeared back

into the mist of the plains and began to gallop along the riverbank towards the herd. Tom could feel the ground vibrating.

His stomach tightened. "Tagus is going to attack the herd," he said. "This is it."

Then he swung himself off the branch and dropped to the ground beside the campfire. He felt a rush of adrenaline. This was the moment he'd been waiting for!

CHAPTER EIGHT

CROSSING THE RIVER

"We have to head Tagus off," Tom said urgently. "The herd is on our side of the river. We mustn't let him cross."

Elenna sprang to her feet and followed Tom as he skirted the edge of the camp, leading Storm by the reins. Silver padded at their heels. The red-faced leader of the cattle drive was fast asleep by his campfire, wrapped up in a thick blanket.

Elenna stooped to pick up a coil of rope from near the fire and slung it over her shoulder. "Which way?" she asked Tom.

Tom gazed out across the plains. Tagus had vanished from view, but Tom knew he must be near. He strained to pick up the sound of hoofbeats, but all he could hear were

the soft sounds of drowsy cattle.

Then the mist parted once more
and Tagus appeared, still on the other
side of the river, his hooves pawing
the ground in fury. His muscles
rippled beneath the shiny black coat
of his horse's body. He flicked his
tail in agitation. His face was square
and handsome, but his hair was
matted and wild.

Tom could see that Tagus was getting ready to attack and was only waiting for the right moment. There was no time to waste. He stepped towards the river's edge. His stomach churned in fear at the thought of those pounding hooves.

"No!" Elenna clutched at his arm and dragged him into the shelter of a jutting rock. "Maybe we should wait for him to come to us."

"We can't," Tom said. "If we let him cross the river, he'll be close enough to attack the herd. We need to stop him from crossing."

"But how?" Elenna asked, a worried look on her face.

"I've left my sword and shield back in our camp..." Tom muttered. "But I've got an idea," he continued bravely. "Give me the rope." He hoisted himself onto Storm, leaving

Elenna and Silver to keep watch beside the river. He hated to bring his horse into battle, but it was the only way he could cross the river quickly enough. Storm gave a nervous whinny and Tom patted his mane.

"I know boy, I'm scared, too," Tom said, reassuring the stallion. "But I know you can do it. You out-ran Ferno the fire dragon, and now I need you to out-run Tagus the horse-man."

With that, Storm reared up and charged towards the river. As he plunged in, Tom gasped. The water was ice-cold and moving fast. Storm fought his way across, but the current was strong and pulled them downriver.

Tom watched Tagus on the other side. The Beast was pacing back and forth, like a lion waiting for its prey. Tom felt fear wash over him. Then,

out of the corner of his eye, he saw something glittering on one of the horse-man's stamping hooves. It was a golden horseshoe.

"Malvel's curse," thought Tom. Somehow, he had to dislodge that horseshoe to break the evil spell and free the Beast.

As Storm neared the bank, Tom tied a quick slipknot on one end of his rope. With any luck, he could lasso the Beast and hold him still long enough to break the horseshoe. He knew it wasn't going to be easy.

Storm panted heavily as they reached firm ground. Crossing the river had taken a lot out of him. Seeing that they had made it safely, Silver let out a fur-bristling howl from the other side of the river.

But Tagus had also seen them, and now he was cantering towards them.

The ground shook with every step.

Tom looked at the Beast, preparing himself for battle. He lowered his arm and swung the rope over his head in a tight circle. As Tagus approached, Tom steadied himself in Storm's saddle.

When the Beast was twenty paces away he stopped suddenly.

Tom had seen a lot of terrifying things during the Beast Quest, but he had never seen such rage in a creature's eyes. He felt himself choke with fear.

Then Tagus charged.

CHAPTER NINE

CHASE TO THE HILLS

The horse-man's muscular body surged towards Tom and Storm, his black eyes narrowed and his powerful front legs kicking as he came within striking distance.

Steeling himself, Tom circled the lasso – once, twice, three times – then flung it at the charging Beast. Got him! The rope landed evenly around Tagus's neck.

Now Tom needed Storm's help to tighten the lasso around the Beast's neck, so it would hold fast. Tom didn't even need to flick the reins. Storm knew what to do. He bolted in the other direction, tugging the lasso securely into place.

Tagus let out a bellow of rage. His

horse-body reared – and Tom was
ripped from Storm's back. He landed
on the ground with a sickening thud.
All the air was knocked out of him.

Before he even had a chance to
think, the rope in his hand jerked
tight. Suddenly Tom was being dragged
across the plains! The grasses tore at
his skin and clothes as he bounced

roughly along behind the Beast. Then
they reached the rocky ground they
had seen beyond the trees. Tom tried
desperately to hold onto the rope as he
was bumped over the rocks, but it was
too difficult. With a powerful jerk, it
was pulled from his hands. He lay
there for a moment gasping for breath.

Then the dark shape of the Beast
loomed up again out of the mist.

Tagus paused for a moment, one foreleg beating impatiently on the rocky ground. Then he reared, thrashing from side to side as he tried to free himself from the rope. His bellows of rage echoed over the plains, and his hooves clattered on the rocks. Tom could hear the cattle stirring. The noise must be frightening them.

Tom stood firmly, facing Tagus and matching his fierce gaze. It was just him and the Beast on the wide-open plains.

With no weapon, Tom did the only thing he could do – he charged.

Tagus did the same.

Beast and boy ran at full speed towards each other. There was no way Tom could survive this. Tagus was five times his size and had ten times his strength. With just one swipe of the Beast's powerful arm, Tom would be knocked out cold.

But Tom had a plan. Just before the two met in a bloody collision, Tom slid to the ground. He slipped right under Tagus's thrashing hooves, grabbing the rope that trailed from the horse-man's neck.

Standing up, Tom was now underneath the Beast's massive body,

holding the rope in both hands.

Tagus pawed at the ground furiously. His eyes glared red with pure hate. He swung a deadly blow with his huge fist.

Tom ducked and rolled out from under Tagus, still holding onto the rope. The Beast reared again. As quickly as he could, Tom ran around the creature. Tagus thrashed and roared, but Tom was too nimble. Before the Beast had a chance to realise what was happening, Tom had wound the rope right around his legs. Tagus wouldn't be able to take a step without falling. And now Tom had a chance to get at that horseshoe without the Beast kicking.

The Beast bellowed with rage. His horse's body twisted and thrashed as he tried to escape the rope, and he swung his enormous arms wildly.

Tom slipped sideways; only his desperate grip on the rope stopped him from falling.

At last, with a fierce snort, Tagus's human half twisted until he could look down at Tom. His black eyes blazed amid the wild tangle of his hair and beard.

Then the Beast raised one arm and struck Tom a crushing blow on the side of the head.

CHAPTER TEN

MALVEL'S CURSE

Tom blinked and shook his head, trying to drive away the dizzy feeling and struggling to keep his grip on the rope. But, with a feeling of horror, he felt it slip from his fingers.

Tom could see the rope loosening around the Beast's legs, and he rolled away frantically, trying to avoid his furious stamping hooves. He fixed his eyes on the golden horseshoe. It seemed loose. If only he could reach out and grab it. One good tug and this Quest would be complete! But the Beast was stamping too angrily. Tom knew he'd never get close enough. He'd be trampled to death first.

Then Tom spotted something moving on the misty horizon.

It was Storm and Elenna! The stallion must have crossed back over the river to pick her up. Elenna was carrying his sword and shield – she must have gone back to the camp to get them. Silver ran beside them, his grey fur bristling in the breeze. They were coming to help!

As they approached, Tagus took his eyes from Tom. He kicked the last of the rope from his legs and howled with fury.

Tom called out to Elenna, "Throw me my sword then spread out! We need to distract him!"

With a huge effort, Elenna threw Tom's sword through through the air so it landed right beside him. Then bravely she rode Storm to one side of the Beast, while Silver darted to the other side, howling excitedly.

It was working! Tagus was confused. He dodged from side to side, snorting and heaving. He didn't know who to go after first. Tom could see the shining horseshoe was clattering loosely on his hoof, but even though the ground was rough the charm refused to drop off.

And all the time they were coming closer and closer to the river, back to the herd of cattle.

"We can't keep this up for ever!" Tom thought.

What more could they do?

They had to stop Tagus before he

crossed the river and scared the cattle
into a stampede – or, worse, killed
some of them.

"Cut us off!" Tom yelled to his friend.
"Get between us and the river!"

Elenna kicked her heels, urging

Storm to go faster, passing right in front of Tagus just before he reached the river.

The Beast was forced to stop for just a moment – and that was all it took.

In a flash Tom slipped the tip of his sword into the glowing golden horseshoe, and twisted as hard as he could.

The horseshoe shot into the air like a firework and vanished in an explosion of bright-blue smoke.

Tagus let out a roar as it disappeared. In that moment, Tom could feel all the Beast's anger, all the horror of his enslavement to Malvel.

"We did it!" Elenna cried. She brought Storm to a halt and patted his sweating neck. The horse's sides were heaving after the long gallop. "Well done, Storm," she said.

Silver let out a howl of triumph and

stood panting, his tongue lolling out.

Tom leaned on the hilt of his sword, trying to catch his breath. Then he noticed a crescent-shaped scrap of shining gold on the ground. A piece of the Beast's magical horseshoe!

"I know what that's for," he said smiling. He picked it up and put it into his pocket.

He looked up at the Beast. Even though Tom knew the spell had been

broken, he swallowed nervously as
the horse-man gazed down at him.
His black eyes were calm now. He
bowed his head majestically to Tom
and Elenna. Then he reached out
with one hand to stroke Storm's nose.

As he did so, Tom spotted
something moving in the shadow
of a rock. A cougar was slinking
towards the herd.

The Beast's head swung round. He

stamped his hooves once, then took off across the river and after the predator. It fled, yelping in terror.

"Tagus can go back to what he's supposed to do," Tom said, watching as the magnificent Beast galloped into the distance.

Elenna nodded. "The herds will be safe again."

"And the people will have cattle to trade with the rest of the kingdom – they'll be able to rebuild the villages that were destroyed," Tom finished. He felt happiness flood him. But he still had one more thing to do.

He pulled the golden scrap of horseshoe out of his pocket as Elenna passed him his shield. He could already see the place where this token would fit – beside the scale of Ferno the fire dragon, the tooth from Sepron the sea serpent, and the feather from

Arcta the mountain giant.

As he slotted the scrap into place,
a sparkling mist curled around Tom's
shoulders. He turned to see Aduro. The
wizard's outline was pale and
shimmering in the early morning light.

"Well done," Aduro said with
a smile. "Thanks to your courage,
another Beast is free."

Tom and Elenna glanced at each
other. Elenna's eyes were shining at

the wizard's praise, and Tom felt he would burst with pride.

"We did our best," he said modestly.

"The whole of Avantia is in your debt," Aduro told them. Pointing to Tom's shield, he added, "I see you found a piece of Tagus's horseshoe."

"Yes! What does it do?" Tom asked.

"It gives you the gift of speed," the wizard explained. "But take care. Use your power only for good."

"I will," said Tom.

"Where do we go now?" Elenna asked eagerly.

"Yes, what's our next Beast Quest?" said Tom.

Aduro turned and pointed north. "You must go back the way you came," he said. "It is your task to meet a Beast in the far north. Nanook the snow monster is waiting for you."

Tom looked to the northern horizon. He shivered as he imagined the icy winds and snowstorms that blew there all year round.

"Nanook is destroying the great ice plains – as well as the rare herbs that grow there, which are used for the kingdom's medicines," Aduro said quietly. "The nomad clans who live there are in grave danger."

Tom felt his hand tighten around the handle of his sword and he raised his shield up to his chest. "I'll save them," he said. "It is my Quest. I must complete it."

Aduro nodded. "You're just like your father," he said.

"Really?" said Tom curiously. "How do you know?"

But the wizard only smiled mysteriously. "Avantia salutes you…" he said, as he faded back into the mist.

Elenna came to stand beside Tom. "We'll do it together," she said, placing a hand on Silver's head. Storm tossed his head and neighed. "We won't give up now."

"Then what are we waiting for?" Tom asked, grinning at his friends. "Let's go!"

But first the four of them made their way back to the camp. There was still one last campfire to enjoy before they began the long, cold trek north.

Join Tom on the next stage
of the Beast Quest

Meet

NANOOK
THE SNOW
MONSTER

Can Tom free Nanook from
Malvel's evil spell?

PROLOGUE

Albin ran across the ice field towards the football, ignoring the painful stitch in his side. He willed his legs to work faster, faster...

His team were a goal down, and it was getting dark. Soon everyone would return to the nomads' camp for dinner and the game would be over. If only he could equalise...

He reached the ball just a second ahead of the goalkeeper and booted it wildly. It flew through the open goal in a shower of snow.

"Yes!" he yelled, and his team surrounded him, whooping with delight.

"Your turn to get the ball," said the goalkeeper sulkily. He wasn't happy!

There was no net in the goalpost, and Albin had kicked the ball so hard that it had landed somewhere in the snow dunes behind the ice field.

"You'd better be careful," said another boy. "The elders say they've seen snow panthers in the dunes."

"Of course I'll be careful," Albin grinned.

He had lived in the icy north of Avantia all

his life and knew the wintery white landscape like the back of his hand – the ice fields, the frozen sea and lake, the snow dunes, and the nomads' camp where he and his family lived. "There's nothing to fear!" he thought.

He ran to the edge of the ice field and scrambled up a snowy dune. From the top there was nothing to see but the hard, white landscape stretching out into the distance, glimmering in the evening light. Albin shielded his eyes against the glare of the setting sun, but he couldn't see the ball anywhere. In the distance he heard his friends shouting and laughing as they made their way back to the camp.

He skidded down the other side of the slope to a narrow icy path that wound between the snow dunes. There was the ball. But...it had been squashed flat. He looked at it, puzzled. What had happened to it?

Then he heard a different noise. A strange, high, tinkling sound – like a bell.

As Albin gazed down at the ball, a shadow passed over him. A huge shadow.

With a sudden feeling of dread, he looked up.

A towering creature, five times his size, stood over him, rocking from side to side on its huge hind legs. Its shaggy fur was thick and white. Blood-red eyes glared down at Albin, and huge, curving, ivory claws sliced the air. Drooling jaws snapped open, showing razor-sharp yellow fangs. The Beast wore a small brass bell on a chain about its neck, but the fur there had been clawed away to reveal raw pink flesh.

Albin was too scared even to scream. He tried to turn and run, but his legs had turned to jelly, and instead he slipped and fell on his back.

The monster stamped one massive paw down on the icy path.

The shockwave jarred every bone in Albin's body. Panic-stricken he scrabbled up, hurling himself at the side of the snow dune. The monster's claws swiped against his side, tearing through his thick clothes to the flesh beneath. Albin yelled with pain. He put a hand to his side and felt warm, sticky blood. Desperately he scrambled up the dune. If he could only get to the top, in sight of the camp, he might be safe…

CHAPTER ONE

THE NORTHERN QUEST BEGINS

"Of all the places our Beast Quest has taken us," Tom said, "this must be the most amazing!" He stood still and stared out at the icy wastes. They stretched into the distance as far as the eye could see, bright shimmering white under a sky of vivid blue. It was late afternoon and the sun was strong.

"It's very bleak," Elenna said, shivering. "But it is beautiful, too."

Her pet wolf Silver pressed up to her, his grey fur speckled with snowflakes and studded with tiny icicles. She hugged him, grateful for the warmth of his body against her legs.

"I'll check the map and see how much further we have to go," Tom announced. He pulled the well-worn scroll that Wizard Aduro had given him from his pocket.

The horse stood like a coal-black shadow against the whiteness all around, and gave a soft whinny as Tom patted his neck. Tom and Elenna could not ride him on the ice fields, as his hooves kept slipping on the snow and ice, so their journey so far had been slow.

"We're close to the northern-most edge of Avantia. We must be nearly at the end of the trail." Tom pointed to the red glowing path on the map that showed them their route. This was no ordinary map. It had magical powers, and had been given to Tom by Wizard Aduro, special adviser to the king. The map had already guided Tom and Elenna to four different places on their secret Quest to rid the kingdom of the deadly threat of the Beasts!

All his life, Tom had heard stories of the Beasts, legendary creatures that dwelled in the deepest corners of the kingdom, protecting Avantia and helping it to prosper. When he was a small child, growing up with his aunt and uncle, he used to think they were fairy-tales. He'd certainly never met a Beast. But then he'd never laid eyes on his father Taladon, either.

Tom still wondered if he'd ever meet his father, but at least he knew now that the Beasts were real. Malvel the Dark Wizard had enslaved them with an evil curse and was using them to spread terror and destruction across the land. One special person had to take on the Quest to free the Beasts and save the kingdom from ruin. King Hugo and Wizard Aduro had chosen Tom. He was determined not to let them down!

He had set off with only Storm, his sword and his shield for protection. But soon he had met Elenna and Silver, and they'd joined him on his Quest. Without them, Tom knew he would never have made it this far. Together they had freed four Beasts from Malvel's curse, and now they were in search of the fifth – Nanook the snow monster.

Many of the rare herbs used in Avantia's medicine grew only in the icy northern plains, but without Nanook's protection, the nomads that lived here could not grow or gather them. Slowly the kingdom was running out of medicine! Tom knew they had to find the snow monster and free her. "While there's blood in my veins," he thought, "I will not give up."

"We'd better get going," said Elenna, studying the map. She pointed to a small cluster of tiny tents, which stood up from the parchment, quivering slightly in the breeze. "It looks as if there is a nomads' camp nearby. Perhaps we can stay the night there. I'm so tired I could sleep standing up!"

"Me, too," said Tom. "Let's go!"

As they set off across the ice once more – Tom leading Storm by his bridle, Elenna and Silver following – a sharp gust of wind blew up suddenly, making them all shiver, even though they wore heavy clothing.

Tom quickened his step. "Come on – the sooner we're somewhere dry and warm the better."

Then Silver stopped and barked twice loudly.

Elenna crouched beside him. 'What's wrong, boy?"

Tom saw the wolf's eyes narrow. A growl was building in the back of his throat. "Perhaps he can sense something," he said. The wolf was often the first to smell danger.

A stronger blast of wind whipped at their clothes. This time it didn't die down. Within minutes it was screaming towards them, and tiny shards of snow and ice stung their skin.

"Don't tell me there's a snowstorm building

up," Elenna yelled over the wind. "A moment ago the skies were clear blue and sunny."

"Not any more," Tom shouted. Now the sky overhead was dark grey and wild with driving snow. "We must keep going and reach that camp."

But with the sun blotted out by snow and cloud, he suddenly realised they had no way of getting their bearings. The map was useless.

"I think it was this way," said Tom, turning into the thick grey and white haze, trying not to panic. He could barely keep his eyes open for the stinging snow. "Or was it the other way?"

"I'm not sure," said Elenna, as the storm grew fiercer around them. "But we'll have to find shelter quickly or we won't stand a chance in this blizzard!"

Follow this quest to the end in NANOOK THE SNOW MONSTER.

Win an exclusive
Beast Quest T-shirt and goody bag!

Tom has battled many fearsome Beasts and we want to know which one is your favourite! Send us a drawing or painting of your favourite Beast and tell us in 30 words why you think it's the best.

Each month we will select **three** winners to receive a Beast Quest T-shirt and goody bag!

Send your entry on a postcard to
BEAST QUEST COMPETITION
Orchard Books, 338 Euston Road, London NW1 3BH.

Australian readers should email:
childrens.books@hachette.com.au

New Zealand readers should write to:
Beast Quest Competition, 4 Whetu Place, Mairangi Bay,
Auckland NZ, or email: childrensbooks@hachette.co.nz

**Don't forget to include your name and address.
Only one entry per child.**

Good luck!

Fight the Beasts,
Fear the Magic

www.beastquest.co.uk

Check out the Beast Quest website for games, downloads, competitions, animation and all the latest news about Beast Quest!

Look carefully at the collector cards that you received free with this book. Do the cards have a secret code on the back? If they do, you can use this code to access special secret rooms on the Beast Quest website. If your cards do not have codes, try again next time – there are twelve cards to collect and you get two free with every Beast Quest book!

DON'T MISS
the next set of Beast Quest books. Sign up to the newsletter on the Beast Quest website so that you will be the first to know when the new series is released!

by Adam Blade

All priced at £4.99

The Beast Quest books are available from all good
bookshops, or can be ordered direct from the publisher:
Orchard Books, PO BOX 29, Douglas IM99 1BQ.
Credit card orders please telephone 01624 836000
or fax 01624 837033 or visit our website:
www.orchardbooks.co.uk
or e-mail: bookshop@enterprise.net for details.

To order please quote title, author
and ISBN and your full name and address.
Cheques and postal orders should be made payable to
'Bookpost plc.'
Postage and packing is FREE within the UK
(overseas customers should add £2.00 per book).

Prices and availability are subject to change.